# Inside the NBA
# Indiana Pacers

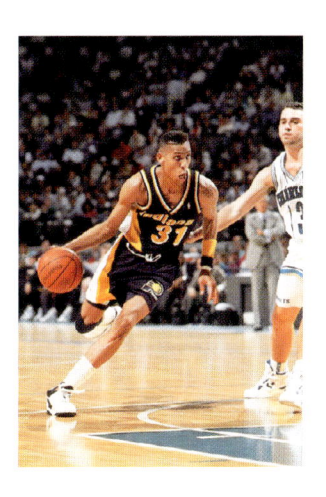

**Bob Italia**

**ABDO & Daughters**
PUBLISHING

Published by Abdo & Daughters, 4940 Viking Dr., Suite 622, Edina, MN 55435.

Copyright ©1997 by Abdo Consulting Group, Inc., Pentagon Tower, P.O. Box 36036, Minneapolis, Minnesota 55435. International copyrights reserved in all countries. No part of this book may be reproduced in any form without written permission from the publisher. Printed in the United States.

Cover photo: Allsport
Interior photos: Allsport, pages 1, 23
     Duomo, page 5
     AP/Wide World Photos, pages 7, 8, 11, 13, 14, 16, 21, 24, 27

**Edited by Kal Gronvall**

**Library of Congress Cataloging–in–Publication Data**

Italia, Bob, 1955-
 The Indiana Pacers / Bob Italia
  p. cm. — (Inside the NBA)
 Includes index.
 Summary: Presents an overview of the history and key personalities of the Indiana Pacers from 1967 to the present day.
 ISBN 1-56239-760-5
 1. Indiana Pacers (Basketball team)—Juvenile literature.
[1. Indiana Pacers (Basketball team)—History. 2. Basketball—History.] I. Title. II. Series.
GV885.52.I53I83 1997
796.323' 64' 09772—dc21     96-40304
                CIP
                AC

# Contents

Indiana Pacers ............................................................................... 4

The Pacers' First Stars ................................................................. 6

Another Weapon .......................................................................... 8

Market Square Arena ................................................................... 9

Retired Uniforms ........................................................................ 10

Welcome To The NBA ................................................................ 11

Transactions ................................................................................ 12

A Reversal Of Fortunes .............................................................. 13

Clark Kellogg .............................................................................. 15

Reggie And "The Rifleman" ....................................................... 17

"The Dunking Dutchman" ........................................................... 20

Playoff Roadblock ...................................................................... 22

Another Trade ............................................................................. 25

Different Team, Same Results .................................................... 26

Breakthrough Year? .................................................................... 28

Glossary ...................................................................................... 29

Index ........................................................................................... 31

# Indiana Pacers

The Indiana Pacers joined the National Basketball Association (NBA) for the 1976-77 season as one of four former American Basketball Association (ABA) franchises to cross over when the two leagues merged. The three-time ABA champions struggled from the beginning in the NBA, posting only one winning season in their first 13 NBA campaigns. After a decade and a half of failure, the team finally began to play .500 ball in the early 1990s. By mid-decade the Pacers have become one of the Eastern Conference's top clubs.

When the Pacers began play in the ABA's inaugural 1967-68 season, they had already been preceded by two Indianapolis NBA teams. In 1948-49, the Indianapolis Jets had compiled an 18-42 record in their only year of existence. The next year the Indianapolis Olympians began play, winning the NBA's Western Division with a 39-25 record. The Olympians folded in 1953 after four seasons.

Basketball has always been popular in the state of Indiana. There is great support for high school teams and for the Indiana University Hoosiers, especially after their success in the 1970s and 1980s under Coach Bob Knight. Professional leagues were always interested in the Indiana market. So when eight businessmen invested a few thousand dollars apiece, the Indiana Pacers' franchise began in 1967 as a charter member of the ABA.

**The Pacers' Reggie Miller drives down the court.**

# The Pacers' First Stars

The first player signed by the Pacers was Roger Brown. Brown became one of the most storied players ever to wear a Pacers' uniform.

After an initial losing season, Indiana ran off seven consecutive winning campaigns under Coach Bob Leonard. In 1968-69, the first of his 12 seasons at the helm, Leonard guided the team to a 44-34 mark. That year's Pacers team scored at a frantic pace, averaging 119.6 points, a franchise record that still stands.

Indiana was loaded with talent, most notably second-year center Mel Daniels, who averaged 24.0 points and 16.5 rebounds and was named the ABA's Most Valuable Player (MVP).

The Pacers struggled at the beginning of the 1968-69 season, winning only 5 of their first 20 games. But they quickly turned it around. They won the Eastern Division title, and beat the Kentucky Colonels and Miami Floridians in the playoffs to reach the ABA Finals. The Oakland Oaks defeated Indiana, four games to one for the title.

The momentum carried over into the 1969-70 season. Indiana ran to a 59-25 record. They finished in first place in the ABA Eastern Division, defeated the Carolina Cougars and Kentucky in the first two playoff rounds, then overpowered the Los Angeles Stars in the ABA Finals, four games to two. Roger Brown threw in 45 points, including 7 three-pointers in the decisive Game 6.

For the season, Brown led the team in scoring with a career-best 23.0 points per game. Daniels boosted his rebounding average to 17.6 boards per game and was an All-ABA Second Team selection.

A realignment of ABA franchises before the next season landed the Pacers in the Western Division. The 1970-71 team finished 58-26 and won the division. The Pacers, however, were eliminated in the playoffs by the Utah Stars. Daniels contributed 21.0 points per game, grabbed 18.0 rebounds per contest (a Pacers all-time best), and won a second ABA MVP Award. He was joined on the All-ABA First Team by Brown.

Mel Daniels drives to the basket in a game against the Kentucky Colonels.

George McGinnis goes up against Swen Nater of the San Diego Clippers.

# Another Weapon

The 1971-72 team's 47-37 record wasn't quite as good, but the Pacers still had what it took to claim a second ABA title. Standout rookie George McGinnis, who had left Indiana University after his sophomore season, was added as another weapon to an already potent lineup.

The playoffs, however, were a challenge. Indiana defeated the Denver Rockets and Utah in back-to-back seven-game sets, then downed the Rick Barry-led New York Nets in six games for the title.

The Pacers repeated as ABA champions in 1972-73. Indiana finished second to the Utah Stars in the Western Division but prevailed once again in the playoffs, besting Kentucky in a seven-game ABA Finals series. McGinnis won the series MVP Award.

Indiana began to slip after those glory seasons. The 1973-74 team logged a solid 46-38 record but fell in the playoffs to Utah.

# Market Square Arena

The 1974-75 squad began play in the 16,530-seat Market Square Arena. Indiana finished the year at 45-39, third place in the Western Division. After a gritty playoff run, the Pacers appeared in the ABA Finals for the fifth time in the league's eight-year history. The Kentucky Colonels and Dan Issel proved to be too strong for the Pacers, however, and took the title in five games.

Prior to the season, the Pacers had traded Mel Daniels and Freddie Lewis to the Memphis Sounds. George McGinnis shouldered the extra burden, scoring a Pacers all-time best 29.8 points per game and sharing the ABA MVP Award with the New York Nets' Julius Erving.

Newcomer Billy Knight, who would become the club's all-time scoring leader with 10,780 points by the end of his career (a mark later surpassed by Reggie Miller), was picked for the ABA All-Rookie Team.

By 1975-76, the Pacers had fallen off the pace. Knight led the team in scoring, with 28.1 points per game, but Indiana closed out the ABA's final season with a 39-45 mark.

# Retired Uniforms

The ABA years not only resulted in the best won-lost record in the team's annals, but also produced many of the greatest players in Pacers' history. Three standouts—George McGinnis, Mel Daniels, and Roger Brown—eventually had their uniform numbers retired by the franchise.

McGinnis played seven seasons with Indiana, from 1971 to 1975 and from 1980 to 1982. A 6-foot, 8-inch, 235-pound forward, he shared 1975 ABA MVP honors with Julius Erving. A two-time All-ABA First Team selection, he finished his career as the third-leading scorer in Indiana history. McGinnis still holds team records for points in a game, with 58, and for rebounds in a game, with 37.

Daniels, a 6-foot, 9-inch, 225-pound center, played six seasons with the Pacers. He was twice named ABA MVP and was a four-time All-ABA selection. Daniels averaged 19.5 points and 15.9 rebounds during his tenure with the franchise.

Brown, the Pacers' first player, spent eight years with the club, consistently averaging in double figures. The 6-foot, 5-inch Brown finished his career as Indiana's second-leading career scorer, and he had the third-highest-scoring night in franchise history with 53 points.

# Welcome To The NBA

After the Pacers joined the NBA (along with the Denver Nuggets, the New York Nets, and the San Antonio Spurs), all of their ABA achievements became history. Playing in the NBA proved to be a rude awakening. The team that had been a dominant force in the ABA found itself struggling as an also-ran in its new surroundings.

The 1976-77 Pacers ended up with a 36-46 record. Billy Knight was stellar, hitting 831 field goals to lead the team in scoring with 26.6 points per game. John Williamson also averaged better than 20 points. Guard Don Buse set a club record by averaging 8.5 assists. Knight and Buse represented Indiana in the 1977 NBA All-Star Game.

Pacers' guard Don Buse takes control as he dribbles around New York Nets' Dave Wohl.

# Transactions

Before the 1977-78 campaign, the Pacers traded away their two All-Stars from the previous season. Knight went to the Buffalo Braves in exchange for Adrian Dantley and Mike Bantom. Buse was sent to the Phoenix Suns for Ricky Sobers.

The 1977-78 team slid to 31-51. Dantley was averaging 26.5 points when he was traded with Dave Robisch to the Los Angeles Lakers in December for James Edwards and Earl Tatum. John Williamson, the team's No. 2 scorer, with 19.1 points per game, was traded to the New Jersey Nets in January for Bob Carrington. Of the players who remained with the team, Ricky Sobers was the top scorer, with 18.2 points per game.

In 1978-79, slight improvement elevated the team's record to 38-44. The Pacers' lineup continued to change, as Roundfield departed to the Atlanta Hawks via free agency, and Billy Knight, by then in Boston, was brought back at midseason in exchange for Rick Robey.

Johnny Davis, a 6-foot, 1-inch guard, led the team in scoring with 18.3 points per game. At the end of the season, California millionaire Sam Nassi purchased the Pacers.

The following season, Indiana struggled to a 37-45 mark. The 1979-80 Pacers tried to recapture some of their former glory by acquiring George McGinnis from Denver. But McGinnis's career was nearly over (he would play only two more seasons).

Billy Knight (25) fights for two down low against the New York Knicks.

# A Reversal Of Fortunes

In 1980-81, Indiana's fortunes turned around. Jack McKinney replaced Bob Leonard as coach, marking the first of many coaching changes over the coming decade. The immediate results were good, however, and the Pacers' 44-38 record was the franchise's first winning mark since joining the NBA. The team got off to a strong 7-3 start and maintained momentum throughout the season, boosted by a seven-game winning streak in January.

Rewarded with their first trip to the NBA Playoffs, the Pacers surrendered meekly to the Philadelphia 76ers in two straight games. Still, things seemed to be moving in a positive direction.

The Pacers' roster recalled the team's winning past. Billy Knight led the club in scoring, George McGinnis had returned, and Don Buse was back as a role player. But although the names were the same, their performances weren't.

Steadier contributors included James Edwards, Johnny Davis, Mike Bantom, Louis Orr, Dudley Bradley, and Clemon Johnson, all of whom saw action nightly as Coach McKinney shuffled the lineup to find a winning combination. For his success, McKinney was named NBA Coach of the Year.

All of the promise of the previous season evaporated in 1981-82, as the Pacers fell to 35-47. The Pacers' silver lining, though, was Herb Williams, a rookie out of Ohio State who grabbed 605 rebounds, his first of six seasons with 500-plus boards.

The Pacers were beginning a lengthy residency in the Central Division basement. Their 20-62 record for 1982-83 was the worst in team history. Only twice during the season was Indiana able to win two games in a row. The Pacers floundered to a 6-33 record over the last three months of the year, including a 12-game losing streak in February and March. Not surprisingly, they drew their all-time smallest crowd during the skid—2,745 fans for a game against the Chicago Bulls on February 16.

Herb Williams shoots a jumper in heavy traffic against the New Jersey Nets.

# Clark Kellogg

Newcomer Clark Kellogg, a 6-foot, 7-inch, 227-pounder and the Pacers' second consecutive draft pick out of Ohio State, was sensational. He led the squad in scoring with 20.1 points per game (ppg) and rebounding with 10.6 boards per game. He made the NBA All-Rookie Team but lost out in Rookie of the Year voting to the San Diego Clippers' Terry Cummings. The Pacers also received strong contributions from Billy Knight (17.1 ppg), and Williams (16.9 ppg, and 171 blocked shots).

The Pacers careened in all directions through 1983-84, ending the year at 26-56. Kellogg and Williams provided courageous performances, but the rest of the team simply lacked the talent to be competitive. Center Steve Stipanovich, a 7-foot, 250-pound rookie out of Missouri, averaged 12.0 points and 6.9 rebounds and made the NBA All-Rookie Team.

In 1983, Sam Nassi, who had owned the team since 1979, sold the Pacers to shopping center moguls Melvin and Herbert Simon. Jack McKinney was released from his contract after the 1983-84 season, and one of his assistants, George Irvine, was promoted to the head coaching position. Irvine had played six ABA seasons with the Virginia Squires and the Denver Nuggets, but he didn't have the answers for the Pacers in 1984-85. They went 3-21 during the final two months of the schedule, including a team record-tying 12-game losing streak, and finished at 22-60.

Clark Kellogg pulls down a rebound in a game against the Philadelphia 76ers.

Once again Kellogg (18.6 ppg, 9.4 rpg), and Williams (18.3 ppg, 8.5 rpg), were Indiana's top scorers and rebounders. But they began to get help from 6-foot, 5-inch guard Vern Fleming, a lightning-quick rookie out of Georgia who contributed 14.1 points per game. Although the results weren't reflected in the win column, the Pacers were putting together the nucleus of a better team.

In 1985-86, Oklahoma forward Wayman Tisdale came aboard as the second selection overall in the 1985 NBA Draft. Williams, Kellogg, Tisdale, Fleming, and Stipanovich were all good players, but they weren't superstars. The result was a 26-56 record.

After a 10-year coaching reign in Portland, Jack Ramsay took over as the Pacers' coach prior to the 1986-87 season. Ramsay engineered a dramatic turnaround, guiding Indiana to their first playoff appearance since 1981.

The team got off to a fast start, winning 6 of its first 10 games. The team held steady through the season, then finished strong, with 10 victories in the final 16 games. The Pacers faced the Atlanta Hawks in the first round of the playoffs. After dropping the first two contests, Indiana claimed its first NBA playoff victory, 96-87, before losing the next game and exiting.

# Reggie And "The Rifleman"

Newcomers Chuck "the Rifleman" Person, a rookie, and John Long, who had come to the Pacers after eight seasons with the Detroit Pistons, were the team's scoring leaders. Person, a 6-foot, 8-inch, 225-pounder out of Auburn, led the team in scoring with 18.8 points per game and was named NBA Rookie of the Year. Williams, Tisdale, Stipanovich, and Fleming all provided double-figure scoring support.

With the 11th overall pick in the 1987 NBA Draft, Indiana chose scoring machine Reggie Miller, a 6-foot, 7-inch guard from UCLA. Miller came from an athletic family. His sister, Cheryl, was once considered the dominant player in women's college basketball, and his brother, Darrell, had been a catcher in Major League Baseball. Reggie Miller had both a delicate shooting touch and a tough competitive nature, and he became one of the league's top offensive threats.

The 1987-88 Pacers finished at 38-44 and out of the playoffs once again. Miller played sparingly as a rookie, backing up Long and averaging 10.0 points. Person led the team in scoring for a second consecutive season with 17.0 points per game, followed closely by Tisdale with 16.1.

# Indiana

Mel Daniels averaged 21 points per game during the 1970-71 season, and grabbed 18 rebounds per contest, a Pacers' all-time best.

At the end of his career, Billy Knight became the Pacers' all-time scoring leader, with 10,780 points.

Clark Kellogg made the NBA All-Rookie Team in 1983.

# Pacers

Detlef Schrempf's rebound total of 780 was third highest in Pacers' history.

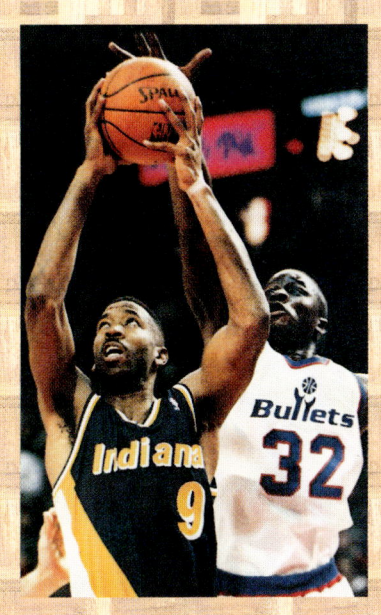

Derrick McKey was named to the NBA All-Defensive Second Team in 1994.

By the end of the 1992-93 season, Reggie Miller had become the Pacers' all-time NBA scoring leader, with 9,305 points.

Pacers' center Rik Smits prepares to shoot over the defense of Washington Bullets' forward Charles Jones.

# "The Dunking Dutchman"

Indiana owned the second pick overall in the 1988 NBA Draft, and added a huge building block in more ways than one. The Pacers selected Marist's 7-foot, 4-inch center Rik Smits, who would develop into one of the league's toughest matchups in the pivot. The 1988-89 season got off to a disastrous start as Indiana lost its first seven games. Jack Ramsay stepped down, ending a Hall of Fame coaching career that spanned 21 seasons and 864 victories. Mel Daniels and George Irvine filled in until the Pacers named Dick Versace as Ramsay's replacement. By the time things settled down, the Pacers stood at 6-23. They never recovered.

In February, the Pacers made two personnel moves. First they traded Wayman Tisdale and a draft pick to the Sacramento Kings for LaSalle Thompson and Randy Wittman. Then they sent Herb Williams to the Dallas Mavericks in exchange for Detlef Schrempf and a second-round draft choice.

The team finished at 28-54, and for the sixth time in seven years the Pacers were last in the Central Division. Williams corralled 29 rebounds against Denver on January 23, the highest Pacers' total since the days of George McGinnis. Smits, "the Dunking Dutchman" from Eindhoven, Holland, scored 11.7 points per game, grabbed 6.1 rebounds per outing, ranked 10th in the league in blocked shots, and was named to the NBA All-Rookie First Team.

The 1989-90 Indiana team started fast at 19-9, and ended at 42-40. Reggie Miller's average of 24.6 points per game was the club's highest mark since Billy Knight's 26.6 in 1976-77. Miller made the All-Star Team, becoming the first Pacers player to perform in the midseason classic in 13 years. He set a team record with 150 three-pointers, smashing Billy Keller's mark of 123 set in 1975-76.

Chuck Person averaged 19.7 points, and Detlef Schrempf added 16.2 points per outing. Schrempf, a native of Germany, had learned basketball as a teen and had played college ball at the University of Washington. A 6-foot, 10-inch forward, Schrempf possessed impressive skills at both ballhandling and passing for a player his size.

Back in the playoffs in 1990, the Pacers ran into the Detroit Pistons, who were on their way to a second consecutive NBA Championship. Detroit disposed of Indiana in three straight first-round games.

# Playoff Roadblock

Bob Hill replaced Head Coach Dick Versace 25 games into the 1990-91 campaign. After a sputtering start, Indiana finished strong, closing out the season at 41-41.

Miller set a new club mark for free-throw accuracy, making good on 91.8 percent of his charity tosses. Schrempf won the NBA Sixth Man Award after contributing 16.1 points, 8.0 rebounds, and 3.7 assists per game off the bench. Miller (22.6 ppg), Person (18.4), and Schrempf were again the team's leading scorers. Vern Fleming chalked up 18 assists in a November 23 game against the Houston Rockets, the top single-game mark since the Pacers joined the NBA.

The Pacers extended the Boston Celtics to five games in a first-round playoff series made memorable by the antics of Person. The cocky forward taunted his more accomplished counterparts throughout the series and backed up his words with 26 points per game, including a 17-for-31 performance from three-point range. Indiana also received strong postseason performances from Schrempf (15.8 ppg) and Miller (22.6), but it wasn't enough to prevent a 124-121 Celtics victory in Game 5.

The 1991-92 Pacers team went 40-42. Four-year veteran Micheal Williams assumed the starting point guard duties and averaged 8.2 assists, the best Pacers' mark since Don Buse's 8.5 in 1976-77. Schrempf (17.3 ppg, 9.6 rpg, 3.9 apg) won his second consecutive NBA Sixth Man Award. The Pacers met Boston again in the playoffs, but without the same fireworks. The Celtics swept the first-round series in three games.

Detlef Schrempf in a game against the Los Angeles Lakers.

Prior to the 1992-93 season, Indiana shook up its roster by trading colorful star Chuck Person, along with Williams, to the Minnesota Timberwolves for point guard Pooh Richardson and forward Sam Mitchell. Once the season began, the Pacers were average as usual, fashioning a 41-41 record. Dale Davis, a 6-foot, 11-inch second-year forward, set a team record for field-goal percentage at .568. He also grabbed a team-high 291 offensive rebounds.

Versatile Detlef Schrempf, in his last season as a Pacer, moved from sixth man to starter and played in his first NBA All-Star Game. For the season, Schrempf averaged 19.1 points and yanked down 9.5 rebounds per game. His rebound total of 780 was the third highest in Pacers' history. Among other accomplishments, Schrempf set a Pacers NBA record by making 22 free throws against the Golden State Warriors on December 8.

Reggie Miller, the team's all-time three-point leader, made 167 treys for the season, tying Phoenix's Dan Majerle for tops in the

NBA, and falling only five short of the NBA single-season record. He poured in a team-record eight three-pointers against the Milwaukee Bucks on April 18. He also scored 57 points against the Charlotte Hornets on November 28, the highest total for a Pacers' player since the team had entered the NBA, and second only to George McGinnis's 58-point effort in 1972-73. By the end of the season, Miller had become the Pacers' all-time NBA scoring leader, with 9,305 points, and he ranked fourth on the club's overall career list (which includes ABA players).

The Pacers returned to the NBA Playoffs, but again made an early exit, losing to the New York Knicks, three games to one, in the first round. Rik Smits came alive in the postseason, torching the Knicks for 22.5 points per game. Miller also stepped up his play, pouring in 31.5 points per game. After the 1992-93 season, Indiana fired Bob Hill and hired Larry Brown as head coach.

Pacers' guard Reggie Miller handles the ball in a game against the New York Knicks.

# Another Trade

Larry Brown's ability to turn clubs around continued at Indiana, as the Pacers came within a few buckets of reaching the 1994 NBA Finals. At the season's outset, however, Indiana fans were skeptical. Days before the opener, the Pacers traded All-Star forward Detlef Schrempf to the Seattle SuperSonics for Derrick McKey.

The team played .500 ball into April, but turned hot as the playoffs neared. The Pacers won their final eight games to finish at 47-35. Then they whizzed through the first round of the postseason with a sweep of the Orlando Magic. In the conference semifinals, Indiana upset the top-seeded Atlanta Hawks in six games.

All of a sudden, the Pacers were a well-rounded team. Rik Smits was accurate inside, and Reggie Miller was accurate outside. Dale Davis and rookie Antonio Davis were hitting the boards, and McKey was providing the leadership. Indiana also received key help in the backcourt from two new additions: veteran Byron Scott and journeyman point guard Haywoode Workman.

The Pacers met the New York Knicks in the Eastern Conference Finals. The Knicks won the first two games in New York, but the Pacers came back with two wins at Market Square Arena. In Game 5, at Madison Square Garden, Miller exploded for 25 points in the fourth quarter, leading Indiana to a key road victory and pushing the Knicks to the brink of elimination. But New York finally prevailed, winning the next two games to take the series in seven.

With his hot shooting throughout the playoffs, Miller catapulted himself to NBA superstardom. In the offseason he was the leading scorer on Dream Team II, the United States squad that won a gold medal at the 1994 World Championship of Basketball.

# Different Team, Same Results

If the Pacers had a weakness in 1993-94, it was at the point guard position. Indiana addressed that need the next season by acquiring former All-Star Mark Jackson from the Los Angeles Clippers. But despite the new addition, the Pacers' season ended exactly as it had the year before, with a loss in Game 7 of the Eastern Conference Finals. This time the spoilers were the Orlando Magic.

The playoff defeat ended a fine year for Indiana. The team won its first division title since joining the NBA and recorded its first season with more than 50 wins (52-30) since the 1972-73 Indiana Pacers of the ABA won 51 games on the way to a league championship.

Rik Smits enjoyed his best NBA season, averaging 17.9 points and 7.7 rebounds, both career highs. Reggie Miller continued to lead the team offensively, pacing the Pacers with 19.6 points per game. He also finished fourth in the league in free-throw percentage at .897, and ranked 15th in the NBA in three-point percentage at .415.

Miller, a starter in the 1995 All-Star Game and a member of the All-NBA Third Team, had some memorable moments, particularly in the wild conference semifinals series against the New York Knicks. In Game 1, at Madison Square Garden, Miller amazingly scored eight points in the final 16.4 seconds to erase a six-point Knicks lead and steal the victory. The Pacers went on to win the series in seven games.

Derrick McKey played a crucial role for the Pacers, placing first on the team in steals, second in assists, and third in rebounding and scoring. One of the league's best defensive stoppers, he was named to the NBA All-Defensive Second Team at season's end.

In the 1995-96 season, the Pacers had another outstanding season, finishing with another 52-30 record, good for second in the Central Division. Reggie Miller led the team in scoring (21.1 ppg), followed by Rik Smits (18.5 ppg), and Derrick McKey (11.7 ppg).

Dale Davis led the way in rebounding (9.1 rpg), while Mark Jackson was the assist leader. But despite their regular-season success, the Pacers once again experienced playoff failure, losing to the Atlanta Hawks in the first round of the playoffs.

Pacers' forward Derrick McKey shoots under the defense of Washington Bullets guard Mitchell Butler.

# Larry Bird Comes Home

In the 1996-97 season, the Pacers were led by Reggie Miller, Dale Davis, Rik Smits, Derrick McKey, and Antonio Davis. Newcomers Jalen Rose, Reggie Williams, and Erick Dampier provided good depth. The Pacers, however, had a host of injuries and finished the year with a 39-43 record, missing the playoffs.

Immediately following the season Larry Brown resigned and took the head coaching job with the Philadelphia 76ers. The Pacers, in a surprise move, hired home-state hero Larry Bird to become the head coach. Bird, the Boston Celtic great, who as a player led his Celtics to three NBA Championships, is happy to be coming home.

Bird was born and raised in French Lick, Indiana, where he led his high school team to a State Championship. In college he led the little known Indiana State University to the 1979 NCAA Final Four and a second place finish. That same year he was named College Player of the Year. "I'm very excited about this opportunity to go back home and coach the Indiana Pacers," Bird said. "Indiana is the only team I wanted to coach, and I am excited about this new challenge and new career."

Basketball fans throughout the state of Indiana are excited about their new head coach. The future Hall-of-Famer is a sure bet to get the Pacers back in the playoffs. From there anything can happen. And with the legend Larry Bird leading the way, it could be all the way to an NBA Title.

# Glossary

**American Basketball Association (ABA)**—A professional basketball league that rivaled the NBA from 1967 to 1976 until it merged with the NBA.

**assist**—A pass of the ball to the teammate scoring a field goal.

**Basketball Association of America (BAA)**—A professional basketball league that merged with the NBL to form the NBA.

**center**—A player who holds the middle position on the court.

**championship**—The final basketball game or series, to determine the best team.

**draft**—An event held where NBA teams choose amateur players to be on their team.

**expansion team**—A newly-formed team that joins an already established league.

**fast break**—A play that develops quickly down court after a defensive rebound.

**field goal**—When a player scores two or three points with one shot.

**Finals**—The championship series of the NBA playoffs.

**forward**—A player who is part of the front line of offense and defense.

**franchise**—A team that belongs to an organized league.

**free throw**—A privilege given a player to score one point by an unhindered throw for goal from within the free-throw circle and behind the free-throw line.

**guard**—Either of two players who initiate plays from the center of the court.

**jump ball**—To put the ball in play in the center restraining circle with a jump between two opponents at the beginning of the game, each extra period, or when two opposing players each have control of the ball.

**Most Valuable Player (MVP) Award**—An award given to the best player in the league, All-Star Game, or NBA Finals.

**National Basketball Association (NBA)**—A professional basketball league in the United States and Canada, consisting of the Eastern and Western conferences.

**National Basketball League (NBL)**—A professional basketball league that merged with the BAA to form the NBA.

**National Collegiate Athletic Association (NCAA)**—The ruling body which oversees all athletic competition at the college level.

**personal foul**—A player foul which involves contact with an opponent while the ball is alive or after the ball is in the possession of a player for a throw-in.

**playoffs**—Games played by the best teams after the regular season to determine a champion.

**postseason**—All the games after the regular season ends; the playoffs.

**rebound**—To grab and control the ball after a missed shot.

**rookie**—A first-year player.

**Rookie of the Year Award**—An award given to the best first-year player in the league.

**Sixth Man Award**—An award given yearly by the NBA to the best non-starting player.

**trade**—To exchange a player or players with another team.

# Index

## A
ABA Finals  6, 8, 9
All-Star  11, 21, 23, 25, 26
American Basketball Association
    (ABA)  4, 6, 7, 8, 9, 10, 11, 15, 24, 26
Atlanta Hawks  12, 16, 25, 27

## B
Bantom, Mike  12, 14
Barry, Rick  8
Bird, Larry  28
Boston Celtics  22, 28
Bradley, Dudley  14
Brown, Larry  24, 28
Brown, Roger  6, 7, 10
Buffalo Braves  12
Buse, Don  11, 12, 13

## C
Carolina Cougars  6
Carrington, Bob  12
Central Division  14, 21, 27
Charlotte Hornets  24
Chicago Bulls  14
Coach of the Year Award  14
Cummings, Terry  15

## D
Dampier, Erick  28
Daniels, Mel  6, 7, 9, 10, 21
Dantley, Adrian  12
Davis, Antonio  25, 28
Davis, Dale  23, 25, 27, 28
Davis, Johnny  12, 14
Denver Nuggets  11, 15
Denver Rockets  8
Detroit Pistons  17, 21

## E
Eastern Division  6
Edwards, James  12, 14
Erving, Julius  9, 10

## F
Fleming, Vern  16, 17, 22

## G
Golden State Warriors  23

## H
Hill, Bob  22, 24
Houston Rockets  22

## I
Indiana University Hoosiers  4
Indianapolis Jets  4
Indianapolis Olympians  4
Irvine, George  15, 21
Issel, Dan  9

## J
Jackson, Mark  26, 27, 28
Johnson, Clemon  14

## K
Keller, Billy  21
Kellogg, Clark  15, 16
Kentucky Colonels  6, 9
Knight, Billy  9, 11, 12, 13, 15, 21
Knight, Bob  4

## L

Leonard, Bob  6, 13
Lewis, Freddie  9
Long, John  17
Los Angeles Clippers  26
Los Angeles Lakers  12
Los Angeles Stars  6

## M

Madison Square Garden  25, 26
Majerle, Dan  23
Market Square Arena  9, 25
McGinnis, George  8, 9, 10, 12, 13, 21
McKey, Derrick  25, 27, 28
McKinney, Jack  13, 14, 15
Memphis Sounds  9
Miami Floridians  6
Miller, Cheryl  17
Miller, Darrell  17
Miller, Reggie  9, 17, 21, 22, 23, 24, 25, 26, 27, 28
Milwaukee Bucks  24
Minnesota Timberwolves  23
Mitchell, Sam  23
Most Valuable Player (MVP) Award  6, 7, 8, 9, 10

## N

Nassi, Sam  12, 15
National Basketball Association (NBA)  4, 11, 14, 15, 16, 17, 20, 21, 22, 23, 24, 25, 26, 27, 28
NBA Draft  16, 17, 20
NBA Finals  25, 28
New Jersey Nets  12
New York Knicks  24, 26
New York Nets  8, 11

## O

Oakland Oaks  6
Ohio State  14, 15
Orlando Magic  25, 26
Orr, Louis  14

## P

Person, Chuck  17, 21, 22, 23
Philadelphia 76ers  13
Phoenix Suns  12
Pierce, Ricky  28

## R

Ramsay, Jack  16, 20
Richardson, Pooh  23
Robey, Rick  12
Robisch, Dave  12
Rookie of the Year Award  15, 17
Rose, Jalen  28

## S

Sacramento Kings  21
San Antonio Spurs  11
San Diego Clippers  15
Schrempf, Detlef  21, 22, 23, 25
Scott, Byron  25
Seattle SuperSonics  25
Simon, Herbert  15
Simon, Melvin  15
Sixth Man Award  22
Smits, Rik  20, 21, 24, 25, 26, 27, 28
Sobers, Ricky  12
Stipanovich, Steve  15, 16, 17

## T

Tatum, Earl  12
Thompson, LaSalle  21
Tisdale, Wayman  16, 17, 21

## U

University of Washington  21
Utah Stars  7, 8

## V

Versace, Dick  21, 22
Virginia Squires  15

## W

Western Division  4, 7, 8, 9
Williams, Herb  14, 15, 16, 17, 21
Williams, Reggie  28
Williamson, John  11, 12
Wittman, Randy  21
Workman, Haywoode  25